MW00887810

This book is dedicated to all the parents
of the Fortnite generation.

ISBN-13: 978-1-7326823-4-4
Devin & Evan series, Volume 2
Copyright © 2018 by Whitney Roban

Disclaimer: There is no relationship or affiliation between the author and Epic Games, Inc.

This is the story of Devin & Evan,
Twin brothers and the best of friends.
They share a love of so many things,
Gaming is NOT where that ends.

Sleep was important to Devin & Evan,
Both boys followed their sleep rule.
They were healthy, playing great basketball,
And they were doing amazing in school.

One day, life as they knew it,

Was to be turned upside down.

They were told about the Fortnite craze,

When their friend Jack came around.

That night they played 'til 11 p.m.,
They had already become obsessed.
When asked if they stayed up too late,
Neither Devin nor Evan confessed.

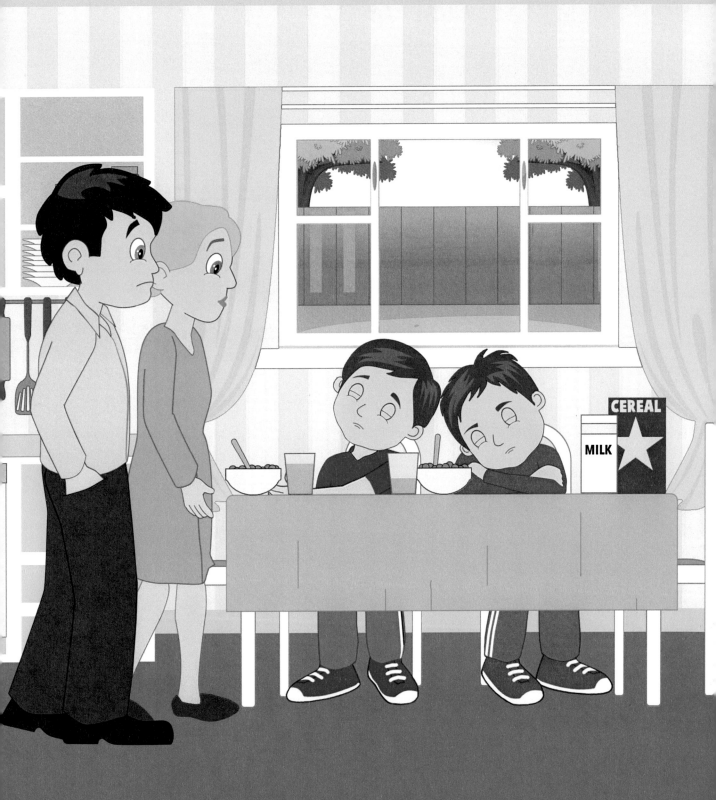

It is 10 p.m. now; they should be asleep,

As their parents walk by their room.

The lights are on; the noise is loud,

And they feel a sense of doom.

They open the door to the bedroom,

Devin & Evan are sprawled on the floor.

The boys are shouting, controllers in hand,

And their parents can't take any more.

Mom and Dad are very angry,

They can't believe their eyes and ears.

They ask the boys why they're awake,

With headsets on, neither boy hears.

Devin & Evan are in big trouble,

But they do not turn off their game.

If they did so during a round,

All their friends would call them lame.

The game is nearly over,

They are very close to a win.

They want to just keep playing,

To unlock the Tier 100 skin.

Their parents shut off the WiFi,

The game comes to a screeching halt.

Devin & Evan are now punished,

As they argue it's not their fault.

The boys finally get into bed,
But they feel that it's not right.
They cannot believe their punishment,
Is a whole week without Fortnite.

Their parents had to remind them,

Sleep is important in every way.

Turn off electronics by 7 p.m.,

To wake up feeling great every day.

Devin & Evan went to bed early,

Not gaming until late.

Each and every day that week,

They felt good and did really great.

Good sleep will always make us,

Healthy, happy, smart and strong.

If you make sure to get enough sleep,

You know you cannot go wrong!

A Note to Parents and Teachers: Why is sleep so important?

Sleep is not a luxury; it's a necessity. We don't just want to sleep; we need to sleep. As human beings, we have the basic biological need to sleep, to eat and to breathe. Healthy sleep is just as important as having healthy food to eat and healthy air to breathe. Every person needs these to survive and thrive.

Sleep affects all aspects of our daily lives. In general, sleep deprivation negatively affects our physical, cognitive, emotional and behavioral well being. More specifically, it has a profound effect on our mood and temperament, our memory, performance, productivity, attention, concentration, problem-solving and processing speed, as well as our immune system and risk for chronic diseases such as heart disease, stroke, diabetes, cancer, and obesity. These negative consequences occur in both children and adults in the home, school, and workplace. There are just no positive results from sleep deprivation.

Most children are not taught about the importance of sleep, neither in the home nor at school. They are unaware of the benefits of sleep, as well as the detriments of sleep deprivation. Using examples from their everyday lives, the goal of this book is to teach children why sleep is so important. Once children understand the value of getting enough sleep, they will happily accept healthy sleep into their lives. Rest assured (no pun intended), it is never too late to teach children healthy sleep habits.

Wishing you all many long and peaceful nights of sleep!

Dr. Roban's 10 Steps to a Well-Rested Family

1. Establish and maintain a consistent sleep schedule, both for bedtime and wake time. Our bodies thrive on consistency.

2. Educate your family on the importance of healthy sleep, focusing on the negative effects of sleep deprivation at home, school, and the workplace.

3. Brief and consistent sleep routines will decrease your family's sleep anxiety. We all feel safe and comforted knowing what will occur at bedtime every day.

4. Accept the amount of daily sleep required to function at our best and move bedtime earlier, if necessary, to get the required amount of sleep.

5. Turn off all electronics at least 1 hour before bed and charge them outside of the bedroom.

6. Make sure every family member gets ample amounts of daily sunlight and exercise. Try not to exercise within 3 hours of going to sleep.

7. Sleep assisted by parents and/or electronics does not produce good quality sleep. We all need to learn to fall asleep and get back to sleep on our own.

8. A healthy diet has a positive effect on sleep. Eat smaller meals throughout the day and no heavy meals before bedtime. No caffeine after 3 p.m.

9. Prioritize healthy sleep to be as important as a healthy diet and exercise. They all affect our physical, emotional, cognitive and behavioral health.

10. In order to get the Zzzz's, follow the ABC's (ASSERTIVENESS in your actions to improve sleep, BELIEF in your family's ability to become great sleepers, and COMMITMENT to healthy sleep).

About the Author

Dr. Whitney Roban considers sleep a necessity, not a luxury, and has helped thousands of families sleep soundly every night. Through her various family, educational, and corporate sleep programs, Dr. Roban provides the education, solutions and support parents need to have well-rested families, students need to have academic success, working parents need to thrive both at home and at work, and corporations need to have healthy and well-rested employees. With a Ph.D. in Clinical and School Psychology, Dr. Roban's unique and invaluable education, training, and experience as a clinical and school psychologist paved the way to her success as a leading expert in family sleep.

Dr. Roban is also the author of "Devin & Evan Sleep From 8-7", the first book in the Devin & Evan series. In this book, Devin & Evan first learn the importance of a good night of sleep.

Made in the USA
San Bernardino, CA
10 December 2018